Into the Fire

by Tracey West

Illustrated by Craig Phillips

Scholastic Inc.

New York   Toronto   London   Auckland

Sydney   Mexico City   New Delhi   Hong Kong

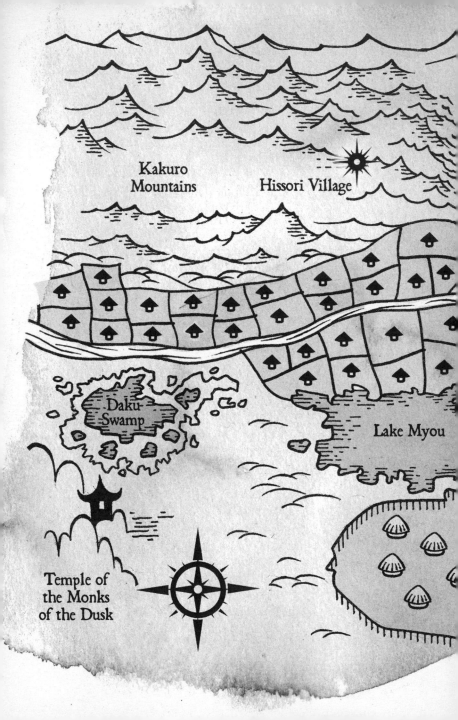

Kakuro
Mountains

Hissori Village

Daku
Swamp

Lake Myou

Temple of
the Monks
of the Dusk

Kagetsu
Mountains

Washi Plain

Forest of
the Yosei

Karibi

Okibi

Hebi River

**Herutsu Province
in the Kingdom of Kenkoro**

For my talented niece Lauren,
who is about to embark on a journey
even more exciting than Hiro's.

— T. W.

ISBN: 978-0-545-16289-0

12 11 10 9 8 7 6 5 4 3 2   10 11 12 13 14 15/0

Printed in the U.S.A.   40
First printing, February 2010
Book design by Jennifer Rinaldi Windau

Chapter One

Hiro raced through the dark tunnel. He could feel the hot breath of the dragon on his back. The promise of sunshine sparkled at the end of the passage. Hiro ran even faster. He had to get away.

Hiro tumbled out of the cave and tripped over a rock. He quickly scrambled to his feet, but it was too late. The dragon's terrible head loomed above him. The beast opened his mouth, and Hiro could see a hot fireball, ready to explode.

Then something soft tickled his face. Hiro spun around, confused. The dragon disappeared. . . .

"Wake up, Hiro! Wake up!"

Hiro opened his eyes, still feeling uneasy from his dream. Just a few hours before, his close call with the dragon had been all too real.

A rabbit with silvery-white hair and bright blue eyes eagerly hopped up and down in front of him.

"Yoshi, it's the middle of the night," Hiro complained. He pulled the cover of his bedroll over his eyes.

"The sun is coming up!" Yoshi said. His pink nose twitched as he talked. "I thought we could practice transforming before we head out this morning."

Hiro poked his head out of the bedroll. Yoshi was right. The first rays of the sun were streaking the sky orange above the distant mountain peaks. Normally, the rising sun was not enough to get Hiro out of bed. But Yoshi's offer was tempting. By age eleven, most ninja had learned how to transform into their animal form, the spirit that lived inside them all. Hiro had done it for the first time just the day before, and he was eager to try again. Being a monkey was a lot of fun.

He threw off the bedroll and stretched his arms, yawning.

"Okay," he said. "I'll practice."

"Hooray!" Yoshi cried. He hopped up, and when he came back down, he had transformed into his human form. He was about a head shorter than Hiro, with the same blue eyes and silvery hair he'd had as a rabbit.

The sudden change surprised him, and he stumbled backward, landing on his back.

"Ow!" he complained. He shook his head. "That keeps happening. Even though I don't mean to, I just change back. I can't control it yet."

"Me, neither," Hiro said. "That's why we should practice. What do you want to do?"

"How about a race?" Yoshi asked.

Hiro grinned. "You're on."

Hiro's family had chosen to camp for the night near

the banks of a narrow stream that ran through a grove of maple trees. The rest of the party was still asleep around the remains of last night's fire. Hiro raised a finger to his lips, nodded to Yoshi, and walked over to the stream. He pointed into the distance.

"See where the stream bends down there? Let's race there and back," he suggested. He drew a line in the dirt with his bare foot.

Yoshi nodded. "You got it. Good luck beating me. I'll wait for you when I get back to the finish line."

"We'll see about that," Hiro replied. "Ready? On three. One . . . two . . . three!"

Hiro closed his eyes.

Come on! he said to himself. *Time to channel monkey power!*

It happened suddenly. Hiro was surprised to feel fur sprouting on his skin and a long tail growing from his back. When he opened his eyes, he saw Yoshi in his rabbit form, hopping down the stream bank ahead of him.

Hiro jumped, grabbing on to a tree branch. His

strong arms propelled him to the next branch. He swung from tree to tree, quickly overtaking Yoshi.

His friend looked up in surprise as Hiro passed him.

"No fair!" Yoshi called up.

"You didn't say anything about a *running* race," Hiro reminded him. He reached the stream bend before Yoshi did. Then he turned around and began to swing back to the finish line.

Yoshi quickly caught up to him. "No way I'm going to let you win now!"

As both boys neared the finish line, Hiro launched himself off of a branch, somersaulting in midair. But during the move, he found himself transforming back into a boy.

"No!" Hiro cried. It was so frustrating not to be able to control his power yet. He landed on the ground with a thud as Yoshi hopped past him.

"I win! I win!" Yoshi cried.

Hiro shook his head. "I was so close!" He smiled at Yoshi, got up, and shook his hand.

Hiro's mother, Rino, walked toward them, carrying a cooking pot she had filled with water from the stream.

"You boys are up early," she said. "Get your packs together. We're leaving after breakfast."

Hiro nodded, and he and Yoshi quickly obeyed. The morning was so beautiful that Hiro began to wonder if the dragon had been just a nightmare after all. The sun shone through the leaves of the maple trees, casting patterns on the ground around them. The air smelled fresh and clean.

Soon Hiro and Yoshi sat around the fire, drinking tea and eating rice porridge with dried apples and plums. It amazed Hiro that his mother's small food pack had managed to feed them all since they left Hissori Village days before.

Their journey had begun unexpectedly. Fujita, an evil ninja with mysterious powers, had come to Hissori Village. His men had ransacked the cottage of Hiro's teacher, old Mr. Sato. Fujita's men escaped with two scrolls that belonged to Mr. Sato—at least, part of two scrolls. Hiro had torn off pieces of them in his attempt to pull the scrolls from the hands of the escaping thieves.

That's when they learned Mr. Sato's secret. He was really the legendary Okuno, the most skilled ninja in all of the Kenkoro kingdom. He was charged with guarding two ancient maps that showed the location of the Amulet of the Sun and Amulet of the Moon. Hiro's family knew they had to find the powerful amulets before Fujita did. With Hiro's friends, Yoshi and Aya, they had found the Amulet of the Moon in a crystal cave, deep in the Kagetsu Mountains. Rino had used the amulet against Fujita and it had only weakened him. He would be back.

Hiro still shuddered at the memory. Fujita's dragon form was so terrifying, it hadn't seemed real. But it was. He knew defeating the dragon wouldn't be so easy to do again.

The same thought seemed to be on everyone's mind as they ate around a newly burning fire. Rino and Yuto, Hiro's mother and father, spoke to each other in hushed tones. Hiro's oldest brother, seventeen-year-old Kazuki, hadn't said one mean thing to Hiro yet, though he usually would have insulted Hiro a dozen times before the last grain of rice was eaten. And Kenta, who was two years younger than Kazuki, was usually full of jokes.

The only person acting like herself was Hiro's friend Aya. She hated mornings and was usually quiet, anyway. Her sleek black hair hung over her eyes as she slowly ate her rice.

Finally, Rino broke the silence.

"Your father and I believe we have eluded Fujita . . . for now," she said carefully. Despite spending two nights in the wild, she still looked as neat as always, with her blue hair pulled back and tied at her neck. "We must be careful speaking. Fujita's spies may be anywhere. So please remember what we say now—we won't repeat it."

She glanced at Yuto. His closely cropped brown hair was streaked with red, like Hiro's, and father and son shared the same golden brown eyes.

"We believe Fujita knows that the Amulet of the Sun is located in the twin volcanoes Okibi and Karibi," Yuto said. "We can reach them in two days if we hurry. Thanks to Hiro, Fujita does not know which volcano is home to the amulet. But we do."

He leaned closer. "The amulet is hidden in the mouth of Karibi. We hope this will give us an advantage. Fujita may choose to search Okibi first."

"He could search both at the same time. He has enough men," Kenta pointed out.

"That is possible," Yuto admitted. "Our best hope is that Fujita is still weak and that we reach the volcanoes first."

"We must leave quickly," Rino interrupted.

Hiro was confused. "How can something be hidden in the mouth of a volcano? Wouldn't it melt?"

Yuto shrugged. "That is what the scrolls say, and the scrolls must be right."

Rino stood up. "Wash your bowls in the stream. We must go."

Hiro, Yoshi, and Aya were the first to finish

eating. They took their bowls to the stream bank. Hiro saw Aya looking up at the trees. Her emerald green eyes looked serious, and a little afraid.

"I had a dream about him last night," she said.

"That's weird. I did, too," Hiro said. "Do you think it means something?"

Aya looked at him. "I hope not."

Hiro remembered his nightmare and shivered.

"Let's go," he said.

Chapter Two

They headed south to the land of the twin volcanoes. The bright spring sun quickly warmed the chilly morning. They moved at a quick pace, without stopping to rest.

For the first two hours, everyone was quiet and serious, thinking about the danger ahead. But as the sun rose higher in the sky, Hiro started to feel more relaxed. It was a beautiful day. Songbirds darted among the trees, and the stream bubbled happily alongside them. More maple trees dotted the countryside, and their leaves waved in the light breeze, almost as if they were saying hello. It was hard to imagine anything terrible happening when things were so peaceful.

Hiro's mom and dad led the group, with Kenta and Kazuki following close behind. Although Kenta and Kazuki were teenagers, right now they whined like little boys.

"Please let us hold the Amulet of the Moon," Kenta pleaded.

"I've already said no, Kenta," Rino said calmly.

"I know Kenta can't handle it. But you should give it to me," Kazuki said. "I can protect it."

Rino stopped walking. She looked directly into Kazuki's eyes.

"It is safe under my protection," she said. "Unless you doubt your mother?"

The question was a challenge.

Kazuki blushed. "No, Mom."

"Then it is settled," Rino said. "Both of you, listen.

There may come a time when one of you may have to wield the Amulet of the Moon. If that happens, I believe you will be ready. But I hope that time never comes."

"Why not?" Kazuki asked.

"You could let us practice with it," Kenta suggested.

Rino shook her head. "Wielding the amulet is a great responsibility. You must have the wisdom to know when to use it. And when you do, you will find your own energy drained."

"But you look fine, Mom," Kenta said.

"I know my strengths," Rino said firmly. "And as your mother, I know yours, too. Now is not the time."

Hiro listened carefully to their conversation. His mother had recovered the amulet only yesterday. He had seen the power of the silver wristband for himself. Rino had used it to drive back Fujita. It amazed him that so much power could come from such a small item.

Yoshi interrupted his thoughts.

"I still don't get it," he said, stepping up to walk beside Hiro. "Only your mom and Kenta and Kazuki can use the Amulet of the Moon?"

Aya joined them. "It's easy to remember, Yoshi. Just look at their eyes. Kenta, Kazuki, and Rino all have the blue-gray eyes of the Gekkani family. They inherited the powers of the sorcerer who created the Amulet of the Moon."

"Oh, right." Yoshi nodded, remembering. "And Hiro and his dad have the golden eyes of the Hinata family, so they can wield the Amulet of the Sun. That's cool, Hiro. I'd like to see Fujita try to blast you with dragon fire. I bet you could totally burn him with the power of the sun instead."

Yoshi made a fist and held his arm in front of his face, as if he were wearing the amulet. "Take that, Fujita. *Pow! Pow!*"

Hiro laughed. "My dad will be the one to get it. I'll probably never even get to touch it."

"That's a lot of power," Aya said. "In the sky, the moon gets its brightness from the sun. Maybe the

Amulet of the Sun is even more powerful than the moon amulet. It might be difficult to control."

"I didn't think of that," Yoshi said. "Boy, I'm kind of glad I'm not you, Hiro."

"Gee, thanks," Hiro said, giving Yoshi a playful punch in the arm. But he knew what his friend meant. Hiro had never really thought about what a big responsibility his family had.

Good thing Dad is going to use the amulet, Hiro thought. *He's a strong tiger. I'm just a monkey. How could a monkey defeat Fujita, even with the power of the sun?*

The woods thinned out with every step the group took. They stopped for lunch when the sun was high in the sky, eating a small meal of bread and cheese under one of the last trees on the tree line. A wide, open expanse waited ahead of them.

"Crossing Washi Plain is the fastest way to the volcanoes," Yuto said as they ate. "But it's dangerous, because there is no cover. We must keep our eyes open in case of an attack."

"Like when those crow ninjas attacked us in the mountain pass," Hiro said. On their way to retrieve the Amulet of the Moon, they'd spotted what appeared to be a harmless group of crows. But the crows had transformed into a gang of ninja who took them by surprise.

Kazuki laughed. "Let Fujita send his crows. I'll crush them in my bear paws!"

"I'll transform into a wolf and swallow them whole," Kenta added, licking his lips.

"What will you do, monkey?" Kazuki teased. "Throw mud at them?"

Hiro's face colored. He was proud of the fact that he could transform into a monkey. So why was it so easy for Kazuki to make him feel bad about it?

Aya came to his defense. "Back in the cavern, this monkey took down an eagle all by himself."

"I didn't notice," Kazuki said as he stuffed a piece of bread into his mouth. "I was too busy fighting off a pack of Fujita's men."

Rino stood up. "This is no time to squabble. Let's

move. I will feel much better when we have crossed the plain."

Yuto nodded his agreement. The group quickly packed up and left the shelter of the trees. Hiro blinked in the bright sunlight. There was nothing but blue sky and green grass in front of them. He thought he spotted the peaks of the volcanoes way in the distance, but he couldn't be sure.

Uneasiness crept up on them all again as they walked in silence. It was strange to feel so vulnerable out in the open.

They walked and walked. But Hiro didn't think they were getting anywhere at all. The volcanoes didn't look any closer, and every time he looked at the sky, the sun had barely moved. At this rate, it would take more than two days to reach the volcanoes.

Sweat trickled down Hiro's forehead, and he swiped at it with his arm. He glanced up at the sun, and that's when he saw them: four birds circling high overhead.

He ran to his parents.

"Mom! Dad! The crows are back!"

Rino and Yuto had already spotted them.

"Those aren't crows," Rino said darkly. She and Yuto exchanged glances.

"Protect yourselves!" Yuto told them. "Run. Hide if you can. Your mother and I will take care of this."

"Why can't we fight?" Kazuki asked.

"Fujita has sent four eagles, and they will be strong—too strong," Rino said. "Whatever happens, continue to the twin volcanoes. You must retrieve the Amulet of the Sun before Fujita does."

Fear struck Hiro like a lightning bolt from the sky. He looked up again and saw the eagles clearly now. Each one had a wingspan wider than Kazuki was tall. Their talons were long, their yellow beaks sharp.

Next to him, Aya quickly transformed. Her body glowed with green light. Shimmering scales covered her skin. In the next instant, she was a long snake, slithering away and blending in with the grass.

Stubborn Kazuki turned into a bear and stood firm, pounding his chest. Kenta took his father's advice. Transforming into a wolf, he raced across the plains.

Hiro turned to Yoshi, who looked as panicked as he felt.

"I can't transform," he said. "Eagles eat rabbits."

"Me, neither," Hiro said. "No trees to swing on."

Hiro scanned the plains for any sign of cover. About a hundred feet away he saw some bushes. It was better than nothing. He grabbed Yoshi by the arm.

"Come on!"

They raced to the bushes, hid themselves inside, and watched the scene unfold. Rino had transformed into a white crane and glided across the sky, leading the eagles away from the rest of the group. A golden tiger streaked across the plain beneath her.

"Dad!" Hiro whispered.

Neither of Hiro's parents could match the speed of the eagles. Two of them soared after Rino, and the others dove at Yuto.

They grabbed Rino first, carrying her off in their

claws. Hiro left the safety of the bushes and raced after her.

"Mom, no!" he yelled.

Kenta circled back toward the battle, and he and Kazuki charged toward their father. The two eagles had Yuto pinned down, and he roared as he fought them off. Kenta leapt at them, striking one on the wing. Kazuki swatted them with his mighty paws.

But the eagles were too strong. They picked Yuto up and lifted him into the air.

"Dad! Dad!" Hiro cried.

Then he froze, stunned, as the eagles carried both of his parents toward the twin volcanoes.

Chapter Three

"They're gone," Hiro whispered.

He felt Aya's cool hand on his shoulder. "Hiro, I'm sorry."

Yoshi walked up, wide-eyed. "Where are they taking them?"

Hiro shook his head. "I'm not sure."

"Fujita knows that your mother has the Amulet of the Moon," Aya reasoned. "And he wants the amulet really badly."

"Maybe he'll let them go once he gets it," Yoshi suggested hopefully.

Hiro wasn't so sure. They had encountered Fujita twice, and he had never been so afraid in his life. The ninja emitted pure evil from his pores; Hiro didn't think he'd let his parents walk away.

Kazuki and Kenta ran up, now in their human forms, their faces flushed.

"We have to go after them," Kazuki bellowed. "They won't get away with this!"

"Didn't you hear Mom?" Kenta asked. "She said to get the Amulet of the Sun no matter what happened. We have to listen to her."

"Kenta's right," Hiro agreed. "I want Mom and Dad back, too. But we have to do what Mom said. Fujita has the Amulet of the Moon now. We have to get to the Amulet of the Sun before he does. That's the whole reason Okuno sent us here."

Kazuki frowned. He knew his brothers were right, but it pained him to admit it.

"Mom should have let me protect the amulet like

I wanted," he muttered. Then he raised his voice. "I'm leading the group now. Let's try to get off of this plain before dark."

"Why do you get to be leader? Because you're older?" Kenta asked.

"And bigger," Kazuki replied.

"Oh, yeah? Maybe your body is, but not your brain," Kenta shot back.

Hiro sighed. "It doesn't matter who leads us. We should move quickly."

Aya and Yoshi were already gathering the packs, which had fallen when Hiro's family transformed. Aya lifted a black bag with straps attached.

"Here's the cooking pack," she said.

"I'll carry it," Hiro offered. He took it from her and hoisted it onto his back. He was surprised at how heavy it felt, and realized how strong his mother must be to have carried it all this way.

The thought comforted him. Both of his parents were strong, skilled ninja. *They'll find some way to escape Fujita*, he told himself.

The group trudged on. Kazuki marched faster than Hiro had ever seen him. Kazuki didn't want to let Kenta lead the group, not even for one minute.

Thanks to Kazuki's determined pace, they reached the edge of the plains shortly after sunset. Hiro could see the twin volcanoes, Okibi and Karibi, rising on the horizon. Even at this distance, he could see plumes of steam rising from each one.

To reach Karibi and the amulet, they'd have to pass through a thick forest of pines.

Kazuki began barking orders.

"Kenta, start the fire! Aya, you make dinner!"

Aya raised an eyebrow. "Excuse me?"

"You're the girl," Kazuki said. "Girls make dinner."

"Is that so?" Aya asked.

Hiro watched Aya's green eyes narrow, and for a moment it looked as if she were going to strike Kazuki like the snake that dwelled inside her.

"I'll help," Hiro said quickly. He nodded to Aya. "There's a stream just over there. Let's go fill the cooking pot with water, like my mom does."

Aya's face softened at the mention of Hiro's mother.

"Okay," she agreed.

"I'll get sticks for the fire," Yoshi offered, dashing off.

Hiro and Aya made their way to the stream. Hiro put the pack down on the ground and opened it up.

"Your brother can be such a bully sometimes," Aya said, shaking her head.

"Try living with him every day," Hiro told her. "He can be nice when he wants to. When I was little, he used to pretend to be an ox and let me ride around on his back. But mostly he likes to call me names and tell me what to do."

Hiro took the metal rice pot from inside the pack and lifted the lid. He was about to dip it into the stream when Aya stopped him.

"Hiro, look!"

The Amulet of the Moon gleamed in the bottom of the pot. The round band of silver was adorned with a silver disc. Without thinking, Hiro reached down to

touch it. A small zap, like a jolt of electricity, tickled his fingers. He pulled back his hand and quickly clapped the lid on the pot. Hiro had forgotten that only his mother and brothers could wield the amulet.

"Mom wasn't wearing it," Hiro said. "Of course! Otherwise, she would have used it against the eagles."

"So Fujita doesn't have it, either," Aya said. "He must be angry."

Hiro nodded. "He's probably still looking for us. We've got to tell the others."

He stuffed the pot into the pack and carried it back to their campsite. Yoshi and Kenta were arranging sticks for the fire. Kazuki didn't appear to be doing anything.

"Come here!" Hiro hissed. "The amulet. It's here inside the pot."

Everyone gathered around and stood in shocked silence as Hiro lifted the lid.

"Mom kept it safe," Kenta finally said.

Kazuki quickly reached in and grabbed it.

"I'll keep it safe from now on," he said.

"It's safe in the cooking pot," Aya challenged him. "You should probably leave it there."

"I'm leading this group, and it's my job to decide what's best," Kazuki said. "Now why don't you be a good little girl and go fill that pot with some food?"

Aya lunged at him. "I am *not* a little girl! I am a ninja, just like you are!"

Hiro and Yoshi held her back.

"We can't fight each other, Aya," Hiro said. "We need to stick together, now more than ever. We've got to get to the Amulet of the Sun."

Aya shrugged off their arms and grabbed the pot.

"I will make dinner, but not because *you* told me to," she said to Kazuki, glaring at him. Then she stomped off to the stream.

Kazuki clamped the amulet onto his wrist. He looked pleased.

"We'll rest for a few hours, then move during the night," he said. "It's too risky to wait until morning."

Kazuki walked off to set up his bedroll. Kenta nodded to Hiro and Yoshi.

"Why don't you two go find some more sticks," he said. Hiro wondered why Kenta wasn't arguing with Kazuki about all this. He seemed strangely calm.

"Sure," Hiro said.

He and Yoshi walked into the woods. Yoshi looked toward the volcanoes.

"I guess we'll get there tomorrow," he said. "What happens then?"

"Um, we climb into a fiery volcano, fight a dragon, get the amulet, and save the day?" Hiro joked. "That can't be too hard, right?"

Yoshi was quiet for a minute. "I was just thinking, Hiro, that you're going to have to get the amulet by yourself. Nobody can help you. You're the only one here who can touch it."

Hiro dropped the stick he was carrying. He had forgotten all about that. With his dad gone, Hiro would have to get the amulet.

"O . . . kay," Hiro said slowly. Suddenly, things

seemed much, much harder than they had a moment ago. "In that case, what happens is we climb into the fiery volcano, Fujita fights us, we lose, and Fujita uses the amulet to become the supreme ruler of the world."

"I think I like the first plan better," Yoshi said.

"Me, too," Hiro agreed.

But inside, he was full of doubt.

Being a monkey was fun. But a monkey wasn't strong or powerful, like a tiger or a bear or a wolf. How could a monkey beat a dragon?

Chapter Four

Hiro had slept for only a few hours when Kazuki woke them all. They moved silently, smothering the fire with dirt and packing up.

The crescent-shaped moon in the sky was barely bright enough to light their way. And darkness closed in on them completely when they stepped into the pine forest.

"I'll transform," Kenta offered. "I can lead the way with my wolf vision."

"You don't need to," Kazuki said. "I can light the path."

He held out his arm and closed his eyes. The Amulet of the Moon began to glow softly on his wrist.

"Maybe you shouldn't do that," Hiro said worriedly. "We know Fujita's looking for it. Besides, Mom said it could drain your energy if you use it."

"First of all, you can't see the light unless you're close, and I'd know if Fujita's men were near," Kazuki said confidently. "It's the best way to get through the forest. Second of all, I'm bigger and stronger than Mom, so my energy won't be drained. And third, I'm leading this group, remember?"

Hiro saw Kenta's eyes narrow as he glared at his older brother, but he said nothing.

They walked single file, first Kazuki, then Kenta, then Hiro, Aya, and Yoshi. Their feet barely made a sound as they traveled over the soft blanket of pine needles covering the ground. The forest was eerily quiet, and the towering trees all reminded Hiro of large black dragons. He hoped their trek through the forest wouldn't last long.

They had traveled for a little more than an hour when Kazuki suddenly stopped.

"What's the matter?" Kenta asked.

Kazuki frowned. "I don't know. I can't go farther. Look."

He stepped forward, but was pushed back by some kind of invisible wall.

"That's weird," Hiro said.

Kazuki tried slamming against the unseen force, but it didn't work. He stumbled backward.

"Let me try," Kenta said. He gave the wall a strong push, but nothing happened.

"It's strange," he reported. "It's like there's a brick wall, but I can't see it."

Hiro, Aya, and Yoshi all touched the wall.

"There must be a way around it," Kazuki said. He walked to the left, feeling the wall as he went.

Aya shook her head. "Don't bother. It's the *yosei*."

"What's a yosei?" Hiro asked.

"My grandmother told me stories about them when I was little," Aya said. "They're the spirits that live in the woods."

Yoshi nodded. "My dad told me about them. They don't like it when people come into their forests."

"Those are just kids' stories," Kazuki said.

"Then how do you explain the invisible wall?" Aya asked.

"Could be a trap set by Fujita," Kazuki replied.

"I think it's got to be the yosei," Yoshi added. "I remember one story that was just like this. A traveler was passing through the woods and couldn't get through. He had to ask politely, and the yosei let him pass."

"Right," Kazuki snorted. He talked in a high, singsong voice. *"Pretty please, can we pass through your forest?* That'll work."

He tapped the wall. "See? Still there."

"I think you have to mean it," Aya told him.

"Kazuki, it's worth a try," Kenta said. "What harm could it—"

"Stand back!" Kazuki bellowed. He held out his left wrist, and the Amulet of the Moon began to glow brighter. "No wall will stand in my way!"

A blinding light shot from the Amulet of the Moon, so bright that Hiro had to shield his eyes. When he opened them again, the light had faded but still glowed faintly on Kazuki's wrist. Incredibly, a stone wall stood where the invisible wall had been. A large chunk of the wall had crumbled away.

Kenta was furious.

"Why did you do that?" he yelled at his brother. "Everyone within twenty miles of here probably saw that blast."

"Be quiet!" Kazuki bellowed. "I solved our problem, didn't I?"

"And you've caused us a worse one," Kenta shot back. "I've been trying not to fight with you, because I know that's what Mom would want. But you've gone too far. You shouldn't have the amulet. *I* should be wearing it!"

Kazuki gave him an angry shove. "It's mine!"

Kenta sprang forward, grabbing the amulet from his brother's wrist. Then he swiftly transformed into a wolf.

Hiro gasped. Kenta was running away with the amulet!

Chapter Five

Kazuki gave an angry roar and transformed into a bear. He ripped off a thick branch from the nearest tree and hurled it. The branch landed right in front of Kenta, who skidded to a stop and charged back at Kazuki, snarling.

"Kenta, Kazuki, stop it!" Hiro yelled.

Both boys changed back into their human forms. Kazuki slammed into Kenta, tackling him. He pried the amulet off of Kenta's wrist.

"Ha! It's mine!" Kazuki jeered, rising to his feet.

But Kenta wasn't giving up. He jumped on his brother's back. Kazuki tried to shake him off, but Kenta wouldn't let go.

"Give it to me! You're going to get us all in trouble!" Kenta yelled.

"I think we're already in trouble," Yoshi said. He poked Hiro in the shoulder.

Puzzled, Hiro followed his friend's gaze. To his amazement, he saw what looked like a hundred pairs of tiny red eyes staring at them from the shadow of the surrounding trees. Hiro blinked to make sure he wasn't seeing things, but the eyes were still there. He shuddered in fear.

"It's the yosei," Aya whispered. "I don't think they're happy that we destroyed their wall."

"So what do we do?" Hiro asked.

"It's too late for politeness," Aya said. "Maybe a gift would work. What have we got?"

"There's a bag of rice in the food pack," Hiro said, taking it from the pack.

"Not the food!" Yoshi wailed.

The red eyes were getting closer. Hiro thought he could hear a faint whisper coming from the trees. The sound sent a chill down his back.

Kazuki reared up, sending Kenta flying. The younger boy landed on the forest ground with a thud. Neither brother noticed the danger they were in from the yosei.

"Hiro, hurry!" Aya urged.

Hiro nodded. He opened the bag of rice and scattered it on the ground.

"Here's some rice for you guys," he said. "We hope you like it!"

The whispering in the trees grew to a rumble. Suddenly, a small army of creatures pounced on the rice. The strange sight stunned Hiro. Each yosei was about as tall as a cooking spoon, with a thin body, spindly arms, and legs that looked as though they were made of sticks. A pair of red eyes shone from each tiny face.

The creatures quickly gathered the rice grains.

Aya and Yoshi each grabbed one of Hiro's arms and slowly moved backward. The scene finally got Kazuki's and Kenta's attention.

"What's going on?" Kazuki asked.

"I'm not sure," Hiro whispered. "But I think we'd better run while we can!"

Nobody argued. They quickly grabbed their packs and ran through the hole Kazuki had blasted through the wall. They crashed through the trees without stopping. Finally, they came to the edge of the woods. Kazuki dropped to the ground, panting. Everyone stopped. Hiro saw that Kazuki had control of the amulet once more.

"What happened back there?" Kenta asked.

"It was the yosei, just like Yoshi and I said," Aya answered. She glared at Kazuki. "If you had only listened to us—"

"Exactly!" Kenta interrupted. "That's why Kazuki shouldn't have the amulet."

He started to move as though he were about to tackle Kazuki again. Hiro jumped in between them.

"Enough!" he yelled. "We're supposed to be working against Fujita, not fighting each other. This wouldn't be happening if Mom and Dad were here." Tears stung his eyes as he thought about his missing parents.

"But they're not here, and I'm in charge," Kazuki said, standing up.

"Says who?" Kenta asked.

"Both of you, quit it right now!" Hiro said firmly. His brothers looked at him, surprised. It wasn't like Hiro to stand up to them.

Hiro wasn't sure how to resolve the situation. But he did know both of his brothers well. Of the two, Kenta was more easygoing, and Kazuki was stubborn. Kazuki would never let Kenta hold the amulet. But Kenta might be persuaded to let Kazuki keep it. Hiro took a breath and spoke carefully.

"Mom and Dad wouldn't want you two to argue," he said. "We should all work together. But somebody needs to hold the amulet. Kazuki, you're the strongest."

Kazuki got a smug look on his face.

"And, Kenta, you're the fastest," Hiro said. "Kazuki stands the best chance of fighting off the eagles if they come again. Kenta, we'll need your speed to aid Kazuki if he's in trouble. So I think Kazuki should keep the amulet for now."

Kenta looked thoughtful. "But Kazuki's not in charge?"

"Mom and Dad are in charge," Hiro said. "Until they come back, we'll have to make decisions together."

That seemed to satisfy Kenta. Kazuki was so happy to have the amulet back, he didn't argue. But that didn't stop him from being difficult.

"Fine, then," Kazuki said. "So what do we do now?"

Everyone looked at Hiro. "I'm not sure," he said honestly. "If Fujita saw Kazuki use the amulet, it's not safe for us to travel. But we can't stop. We have to reach the volcanoes."

"I could transform into a rabbit," Yoshi suggested. "I could scout ahead and see if there's a trap."

"Good idea," Kazuki agreed.

Hiro had another thought. "Kenta, maybe you should transform into your wolf and go with him, just in case there's trouble."

Kenta nodded. "Sure."

Hiro felt pretty good about the plan. Besides keeping Yoshi safe, it would probably be good for Kenta and Kazuki to be apart for a little while.

It was still dark. Now that they were out of the forest, the treeless landscape was covered with a mix of rocks and low-growing plants. A few small hills blocked their view of the volcanoes in the distance.

Aya pointed to a boulder. "We can take cover there while Kenta and Yoshi are gone."

"Sounds good," Hiro said.

Kenta and Yoshi transformed and headed up the hill on their scouting mission, while Hiro, Aya, and Kazuki made their way to the boulder. They decided to take turns standing guard while the others slept.

"I'll take the first shift," Hiro offered.

Kazuki didn't bother to unpack his bedroll. He

stretched out on the grass and within seconds was snoring away. Hiro knew that using the amulet had most likely drained his energy, but Kazuki would never admit it.

Aya sat cross-legged against the boulder. She studied Hiro for a moment.

"You're a good leader, Hiro," she said.

Hiro felt himself blushing. "I'm not a leader. Mom and Dad are." He felt the hot tears behind his eyes again.

48

"We'll find them," Aya said.

"I hope so," Hiro said softly.

He gazed up at the starry sky. His parents could be anywhere, anywhere at all.

Chapter Six

Hiro was sleeping when he felt someone shake him awake. Aya was leaning over him.

"Hiro, they're back," she said.

Hiro rubbed his eyes. The morning sky was just starting to brighten. Kenta and Yoshi sat cross-legged in front of him. They were munching on dried apples. Kazuki leaned against the boulder, watching them.

Yoshi's stomach growled. "I wish we didn't have to

give those yosei our rice," he complained. "Couldn't we have thrown them my socks or something?"

"Never mind that," Hiro said. "What did you find?"

"Four of Fujita's ninja," Kenta answered. "I didn't see Mom and Dad. The ninja had set up camp and looked settled down for the night. I don't think they saw the light from the amulet, or they would have been on the move."

Kazuki punched his right fist in his left palm. "It's five against four. We can take them."

"Not if they can turn into eagles," Yoshi pointed out.

Hiro was thoughtful. "Maybe we can learn something from them," he said.

"What do you mean?" Kazuki asked.

"If we can get close enough, we can find out if they know where to find the Amulet of the Sun—or what's happened to Mom and Dad," Hiro said.

Kenta shook his head. "They're camped out at the bottom of a hill. They'd spot us coming down it."

"They won't spot me," Aya said. "They won't even hear me."

Kenta looked surprised. "Yeah, you're right."

"Then it's settled," Hiro said. "We should go now."

It took an hour to get to the camp. Kenta and Yoshi led them to a small hill. When they neared the top, they lay down on their bellies and slowly crawled up.

The four men below were clad in black jumpsuits. It looked like they were breaking up camp.

"I'd better hurry," Aya said. She closed her eyes and transformed into a snake in a shower of glittering green light.

Hiro watched as Aya slithered down the hillside. In seconds she blended in with the green grass, and he couldn't see her.

The four ninja had gathered in a circle. Hiro saw a glowing ball of light appear between them. Then an image began to form in the glow—a face. A thin face with dark eyes and a thin black mustache and beard.

"Fujita," Hiro whispered. "Quick, get back!"

Everyone crawled back down the other side of the hill as quickly as they could.

"Do you think he saw us?" Hiro asked.

"I'm not sure," Yoshi said. "What was that, anyway? Is he there? Did he lose his body or something?"

"He's communicating with them somehow," Kenta guessed. "I think he's somewhere else."

"Let's hope Aya doesn't get caught," Kazuki said.

"Aya's quiet," Hiro said confidently. "She won't be seen."

Hiro hoped he was right. They waited anxiously for Aya to return. Minutes passed, and then finally Hiro saw her green form slithering toward them.

"We were jussst in time," she told them. "Fujita hasss a magical way to communicate with hisss men. I learned a lot."

"Do you think maybe you could transform back?" Yoshi asked. "It's kind of weird, talking to a snake."

"Yesss," Aya hissed. In the next moment, she was human once more.

"We should keep moving," she said. "I'll tell you what I found out as we walk."

They quickly left the hillside.

"So what did Fujita say?" Hiro asked.

"He is setting up camps all around the perimeter of the volcanoes," Aya explained. "He's not sure which volcano the amulet is in. He's hoping we'll lead him to it."

Hiro nodded. "Just like Dad said."

"Fujita talked about your mom and dad," Aya said. "He said they're being held at a camp on the west side of the Okibi volcano. He's got them tied up so they can't escape. But it sounds like they're fine."

They're fine. The words slammed right into Hiro's heart and filled him with hope.

"I could find the camp," Yoshi said. "My rabbit teeth are sharp. I could sneak in and untie them."

"That's a great idea," Hiro said. "I'll go with you."

"No, Hiro," Kazuki said firmly. "You need to go to Karibi and retrieve the Amulet of the Sun. We're running out of time."

Hiro knew Kazuki wasn't being bossy—he was right. But he wanted to help his parents so badly.

"Shouldn't we get Mom and Dad first, so Dad can rescue the amulet?" Hiro asked.

"I hate to say it, but Kazuki's right," Aya admitted. "Fujita's men may reach the volcano before we do. We have to hurry."

"How are we going to get past them?" Kenta asked.

Kazuki stopped walking. "I know a way," he said.

He took the Amulet of the Moon off his wrist and handed it to Kenta. The younger boy looked surprised.

"Why are you giving the amulet to me now?" Kenta asked.

"Hiro's right. You're faster," Kazuki said. "And Fujita probably thinks I have the amulet because I'm the oldest. We can use that to throw him off."

Hiro knew what his brother was thinking. "We can split up."

"Exactly," Kazuki said. "Yoshi, Aya, and I will head

for Okibi. Kenta and Hiro will go to Karibi. Kenta, you'll need to use the Amulet of the Moon if Fujita catches up to you."

Kenta nodded. "That's a good plan."

"Do I have to go with you?" Aya asked Kazuki.

"We may need your stealth to break into the camp where my parents are held," Kazuki said. "And Hiro and Kenta have a better chance of slipping past Fujita's men if there are only two of them."

Aya seemed satisfied with the answer. At least Kazuki had noticed her strengths instead of giving her a job just because she was a girl.

Hiro was impressed. Kazuki could be a pretty good leader when he wasn't being bossy.

He looked up at the two volcanoes. The steam rising from them reminded him of the hot, foul-smelling smoke that poured from Fujita's dragon nostrils. The last thing he wanted to do was face that again. A feeling of pure terror washed over him for a moment—the same feeling he'd had in his nightmare—and he shuddered.

But this wasn't about what he wanted. He was a ninja, a member of the Hinata family, and this was his duty.

"Let's get moving," he said. "There's no time to waste."

Chapter Seven

Hiro adjusted the packs on his back and trudged along, grateful for the cool spring air. Beside him, Kenta kept glancing down at the Amulet of the Moon on his wrist. He noticed Hiro watching him.

"I wanted it so badly that I fought Kazuki for it. But now that I have it, I'm nervous," Kenta admitted. "I saw what happened when Mom used it. It's powerful. What if I can't handle it?"

Hiro was a little surprised by his brother's

admission. Kenta always seemed so sure of himself.

"Mom said you could handle it if you had to," Hiro reminded him. "She doesn't lie."

"No, she doesn't," Kenta agreed. "Thanks, Hiro."

They had parted ways with Kazuki, Yoshi, and Aya a few hours before. Hiro knew he should have felt exhausted. He hadn't had much sleep or food in the last twenty-four hours. But somehow he felt energized.

The twin volcanoes loomed before them, but now that they were closer, Hiro could see that the slopes were not as steep as they had once seemed. Clouds of white steam poured from hot springs that were scattered around the base of the volcanoes.

The twin volcanoes were nearly the same size. Okibi was the closest to them, while Karibi was farther south. The others were already out of sight as they headed to the west side of Okibi to find Hiro's parents.

It felt strange traveling with only Kenta by his side. When they first set out from Hissori Village, there were seven of them. Now there were two.

"Are you sure we're doing the right thing?" Hiro
asked. "Maybe we should have stuck together. We'd
have a better chance of defeating Fujita with five
ninja fighting."

Kenta thought for a minute. "I think we did the
right thing," he said finally.

"But . . . I'm just a monkey," Hiro said. "Fujita is a
dragon. How can a monkey beat a dragon?"

It felt good to say out loud what had been worrying

him since his parents had been captured.

Kenta reached out and ruffled his hair. "You're
not just a monkey," he said, smiling. "You're Hiro."

"Come on, be serious!" Hiro protested.

"I am," Kenta told him. "I've been thinking about
all this, too. There's a reason our family was chosen
to protect the amulets, Hiro. I don't know what that
is. But I think we just have to trust it. You know?"

"I guess," Hiro said. But he wasn't so sure. How
could he trust what he didn't understand?

Soon they reached the hot springs at the foot of

the volcano. The steam from the springs felt warm on Hiro's face. As they neared, Kenta abruptly threw an arm in front of Hiro.

"Stop!" he whispered, crouching down and pointing toward the springs. "I see something up ahead. It could be Fujita's men."

Hiro followed Kenta's gaze. A small group of hunched-over figures sat in the springs. It took Hiro a moment to recognize them.

"Those aren't ninja—they're monkeys," Hiro said.

Kenta frowned. "They could be ninja in disguise."

"I don't think so," Hiro said. He didn't know how he knew. It was just a feeling he had deep inside.

Without realizing he was doing it, Hiro slowly walked toward the springs. These monkeys were different from monkeys he had seen before. Their thick fur was a tan color streaked with white. They had bright pink faces. But somehow Hiro felt he knew them.

You do know us, Hiro.

He quickly looked around. Had someone spoken?

Maybe Kenta was right after all.

Don't be afraid, Hiro.

One of the monkeys was looking right at him. It was almost as if the monkey was speaking to him. But that couldn't be. Could it?

I am the spirit of the monkey, Hiro, came the reply. *The spirit in all of us here. Including you.*

A monkey was speaking to him! Or a monkey spirit, anyway. He decided he might as well talk back.

"Can you help me defeat Fujita?" Hiro asked.

We can. We are with you, Hiro. You are not one monkey. You are many. The spirit of all monkeys lives inside you. Connect with us, and we can help you.

"Can many monkeys defeat a dragon?" Hiro asked.

We are with you, Hiro. . . .

Kenta shook him by the shoulders. "Hiro, are you okay?"

Hiro felt as if he was waking from a dream. "Um, yeah," he said. "It's kind of a . . . monkey thing."

Kenta seemed to respect that. "If your monkey thing is over, we should start climbing."

Hiro followed his brother up the slope of the volcano. The climb wasn't as difficult as Hiro thought it would be. The sides of the volcano gently sloped up to the crater.

Still, it was a good distance, and it took them more than an hour to reach the top. Hiro was sweating by the time the crater came into view. He untied the sash around his waist and wrapped it around his head to keep the sweat from falling into his eyes. Kenta climbed ahead of him to the crater's edge.

"Dad said the Amulet of the Sun was in Karibi's mouth," Hiro said. "But how can that be? Isn't there bubbling lava and stuff down there?"

"There is," Kenta said. "But that's not all. Come look."

Hiro joined his brother. A few feet down, he saw a narrow bridge made of wooden slats that stretched from one side of the crater to the other. Hundreds of feet below the bridge, orange lava bubbled and churned. And in the center of the bridge rested a gold wristband adorned with a gold disc.

"The Amulet of the Sun," Hiro said. "Dad was right."

Kenta grinned and slapped Hiro on the back. "Looks like we beat Fujita to it," he said. "Time to take a walk, little brother. You ready?"

Hiro looked at the rickety bridge, then down at the lava. One wrong step and he'd plummet into the fire below.

"I'll never be ready for this," Hiro said. "So I might as well go now."

He closed his eyes and pictured the monkeys at the hot springs.

Okay, monkeys. If you're in there, help me out.

He jumped into the air.

"Monkey power!"

Chapter Eight

Hiro landed on the bridge in his monkey form. The bridge rocked back and forth under him. He knew he'd need to be light and agile to get across, and he had great balance when he was a monkey.

"Pretty cool," Kenta said. "I didn't get a good look at you before."

Hiro looked up at his brother and said, "Thanks." He took a deep breath. "Okay. Here I go."

He got down on all fours and carefully crawled

farther onto the bridge, which continued to rock under his weight. He caught a glimpse of the red-hot lava below and quickly shifted his gaze.

"Don't look down. Don't look down," he muttered. Instead, he locked his eyes on the golden amulet in the center of the bridge. It wasn't that far, really. But from Hiro's point of view, it could have been miles away.

Slow and steady, Hiro told himself. *I'm almost there. Grab the amulet, and then we can get out of here.*

He kept slowly making his way across the bridge. The heat was almost unbearable, and being covered in fur didn't help.

Soon he was just a few feet away from the amulet. A few more steps and he could reach out and grab it.

"Hiro! Look out!" Kenta yelled.

The sound of his brother's voice startled him. He jumped up involuntarily, and the bridge lurched beneath him, tipping him over the side.

Thinking quickly, he grabbed on to the edge and pulled himself up. His heart was pounding.

"Kenta, don't scare me like that!" he yelled. "I almost—"

Hiro froze. High above, a huge winged dragon was flying toward them. His glistening purple scales shimmered in the sunlight. His large, leathery wings flapped as he flew.

"Fujita," Hiro whispered. "It's all over."

For a second, he didn't know what to do.

But Kenta was ready to fight. He lifted his arm, and the Amulet of the Moon began to glow.

"You'd better stand back if you know what's good for you!" Kenta yelled. Hiro could hear the fear in his brother's voice.

Fujita dove at Kenta, extending one long, curved talon.

Hiro saw Kenta fall backward. He looked up at Fujita. The dragon held the Amulet of the Moon in his claw!

Hiro started to panic. How was Fujita holding the

amulet? Hiro remembered the jolt that had shocked his hand when he tried to touch it. Was Fujita using some kind of magic? And could he use the amulet against them?

Fujita circled back around. Hiro felt glowing red eyes on him as the dragon readied to grab the other prize, the Amulet of the Sun.

Kenta reacted quickly.

"That belongs to my family!" he yelled. He leapt up, turning into a wolf in midair just as Fujita flew by. He grabbed hold of the dragon's long tail.

Fujita roared and turned to look. Kenta clung to the tail tenaciously. The he opened his mouth and, snarling, chomped down into the glossy scales.

The dragon screamed and lashed again. Kenta climbed up his back and bit the dragon once more. Fujita's wings stopped flapping for a second, and he plummeted into the crater.

Kenta jumped off his back and landed on the volcano's rim. He looked down in time to see Fujita slamming into the bridge. The ropes anchoring the

bridge to the crater walls broke away on one side, and the bridge swung down.

The motion sent Hiro flying.

"Help!" Hiro yelled.

Chapter Nine

As soon as he uttered the cry, Hiro knew it was senseless. Nobody could help him. He had to do this himself.

He reached out and grabbed the edge of the bridge. Tremors from deep within the volcano caused the loose bridge to shake up and down. Hiro held on with all his strength.

Suddenly, he remembered—the Amulet of the Sun! The gold band was sliding down the wood slats right toward him. He freed one hand so he could catch it.

Whoosh! The bridge flapped up again, tossing the amulet into the air. It flipped over a few times and then began to fall back toward the crater.

Hiro reached out, but he couldn't stretch far enough. Fujita swooped back up from the crater, and Hiro realized with horror that the dragon was about to pluck the amulet right out of the air.

That couldn't happen. Hiro had to stop him, no matter what.

He launched himself off the bridge, somersaulting in the air. He quickly grabbed the wristband before Fujita could get to it.

"Yes!" Hiro cheered.

But now the bridge was too far away to grab. Panic set in as he realized he was seconds away from plummeting into the boiling lava.

A loose rope flapped behind him. Hiro couldn't reach it with his arms. He closed his eyes, bracing himself for what was to come.

We are with you, Hiro. We can help.

"Huh?" Hiro opened his eyes and realized that his tail had gripped the rope and was wrapping around it. Hiro had forgotten he even had a tail!

The rope swung back to the opposite side of the crater. Hiro scrambled around and grabbed the rope with his free hand to steady himself.

Fujita roared in fury. He plunged toward Hiro. Hiro quickly slipped the Amulet of the Sun around his wrist and began to climb the rope up to the top of the crater.

He could feel the dragon's hot breath on his back, just like in his dream. Pure fear propelled him upward.

Suddenly, Fujita let out an angry scream. Hiro turned to look.

A beautiful white crane soared toward Fujita. She gripped the silver Amulet of the Moon in her talons and ripped it from the dragon's grasp.

"Mom!" Hiro cried out. She was safe!

Fujita was furious. He lunged at Rino, and Hiro

realized his mother wasn't fast enough to get away. He had to help her. He scanned the edge of the volcano and saw Kenta sprawled out, weakened from his battle with Fujita. It was up to Hiro now.

That familiar feeling of doubt rose inside him.

You're just a monkey. What can you do?

As soon as he had the thought, he realized what the voice at the springs had been trying to tell him. Moments ago, he had connected to the monkey spirits and they had reminded him to use his tail. He wasn't alone. The spirit of all monkeys really did live inside him— he could feel it. Knowing that made him feel less afraid.

"Okay, monkeys," Hiro said under his breath. "Let's go!"

Hiro jumped into the crater.

"Monkey power!"

He latched on to Fujita's claw. The dragon growled and tried to shake him off. But Hiro held on.

Then, suddenly, Hiro transformed back into a boy.

The change startled him, and he almost lost his grip. Holding on to Fujita wasn't easy in his human body.

"This is the end, for you and for all of Kenkoro," Fujita growled in a low and sinister voice. "No mere boy can stop me. A boy who turns into a monkey. Ha!"

"I am not just one monkey," Hiro replied. "I am many monkeys!"

He looked at the gold band on his wrist. Hiro wasn't sure how to use it, or even if he could. But he had to try. He held up his arm.

"With the power of the sun, I will defeat you!" Hiro yelled with all his might.

Fujita's angry roar shook his whole body, and Hiro almost fell off again. But he didn't let go. He pointed the amulet at Fujita, concentrating all of his energy on it.

The band lit up with a soft glow that became brighter and brighter until it exploded in a mass of golden light.

Then his stomach dropped and he felt himself falling. Panic rose inside him as he realized he was no longer holding on to Fujita's claw. He opened his eyes and saw that the dragon had transformed back into a ninja and had fallen onto the crater's edge.

Hiro wasn't so lucky. He plummeted toward the lava now, with no tail to help him.

At least Fujita won't get the amulet, he thought. Whatever happened, he hoped it would be fast.

He looked away from the lava to see a welcome sight. Hiro's mother sped toward him, propelled through the air by her large, strong wings. Rino swooped down, caught him, and carried him to safety.

Back on the volcano's edge, an orange tiger bounded toward Fujita's limp form. Hiro's heart jumped. His dad was all right!

Before Yuto could reach Fujita, four eagles descended from the sky. They lifted Fujita's body and carried him away.

Rino dropped Hiro on the side of the volcano next to Kenta. His brother looked dirty and a little bruised, but okay. Kenta smiled at him.

"Nice job out there," he said. "You did it."

Hiro looked at the Amulet of the Sun gleaming on his wrist. A grin spread across his face.

"You're right," he said. It was almost too hard to believe. "I did it!"

He closed his eyes, and silently thanked the monkey spirit.

Somehow, Hiro knew he would get the message.

Chapter Ten

"May I have more noodles, please?" Yoshi asked.

"Yoshi, that's your third bowl," Rino said, shaking her head.

"I can't help it," Yoshi said. "Hiro gave all our rice to some forest spirits."

A small man with a long, white beard and wrinkled face chuckled. "You may have more noodles, Yoshi," Mr. Sato said.

The old man stood up and took Yoshi's bowl from

him. Using his cane, he walked to the wood stove in the corner.

Hiro sat cross-legged on the floor and looked around Mr. Sato's small cabin. It had taken them nearly four days to get back to Hissori Village. Hiro had been so wiped out from using the amulet that Kazuki had carried him on his back the first day.

When they finally arrived, they headed straight for Mr. Sato's home. They knew the ninja master would be eager for a report of their journey. Strangely, the old man had a large pot of noodles ready when they arrived, as though he knew they were coming.

Mr. Sato handed Yoshi's bowl back to him.

"You three dealt wisely with the yosei," Mr. Sato said. "Had you not given up the rice, you might still be in that forest."

Hiro shivered at the memory of the creepy creatures.

"Now tell me," Mr. Sato said. "What happened after Hiro and Kenta went off on their own?"

"I led Yoshi and Aya to the camp where Mom and Dad were held," Kazuki bragged.

"We almost got lost," Aya pointed out. "If it wasn't for Yoshi—"

"And when we got there, I fought off the ninja guards," Kazuki interrupted her.

"That part is true," Yoshi admitted. "But then Aya and I snuck into the tent where Rino and Yuto were being held. I chewed through some ropes to set them free."

"And we're grateful you did," Rino said. "Yuto and I are faster in our animal forms, so we transformed and raced to Karibi so Yuto could get the Amulet of the Sun."

Yuto grinned. "Apparently, we didn't need to rush. Hiro did just fine on his own."

Hiro blushed. "I wasn't on my own. You should have seen Kenta. He was amazing, attacking Fujita like that. And then Mom saved me from falling. And then, of course, there were all those monkeys."

Kenta laughed and shook his head. "Hiro had some kind of mystical monkey experience. He won't stop talking about them."

Mr. Sato nodded. "Ah, that is very good, Hiro."

Hiro held up his bare wrist. "Anyway, I'm glad Dad has the amulet now. It's a big responsibility."

Rino and Yuto presented the amulets to Mr. Sato, bowing. "And now they are in your good care," Rino said.

But Mr. Sato shook his head. "The care of the amulets belongs to the Hinata family. Hiro is right—it is a big responsibility. But it is the responsibility of your family from now on."

"But how can we keep them safe?" Hiro asked. "Won't Fujita come looking for them?"

"It interests me that Fujita was unable to remain in dragon form when you used the Amulet of the Sun," Mr. Sato said. "It is possible that the use of the amulet has stripped him of some of his powers. I do not know for sure. We must always think of Fujita as a threat. However, you have defeated Fujita twice already. The amulets are in good hands."

"What if somebody else wants the power of the amulets?" Aya asked.

"Somebody worse," Yoshi added.

Mr. Sato chuckled. "It is difficult to imagine

anyone more terrifying than Fujita, but anything is possible," he said. "Whatever happens, I trust that you will all know what to do."

Yoshi stood up. "I'd better go see my mom. I'm sure she's worried about me."

"I'd better go, too," Aya said.

Yoshi nodded to Hiro. "Want to race me there?"

"Sure," Hiro replied.

"I can race, too, you know," Aya said. "Snakes can move faster than you think."

"Hiro, don't be too long," Rino said. "We all need some rest—and a good bath."

"Just to Yoshi's house, Mom," Hiro promised. "I'll come straight home."

The three young ninja headed out into the sunshine.

"No swinging from trees this time," Yoshi said.

Hiro shook his head. "No way. I'm a monkey. That's what we do."

Yoshi shrugged. "All right. I'll beat you, anyway."

"Don't count me out," Aya said.

"All right, then," Hiro laughed.

The three friends transformed, and soon a snake, a rabbit, and a monkey prepared to race through the winding streets of the village.

"One . . . two . . . three . . . *go!*"

#1 Enemy Rising

Hiro had heard stories about Fujita. No ninja who had faced him had lived to tell about it. And now Fujita seeks an **ancient amulet** that would bring him power over the Kenkoro kingdom. Hiro and the rest of the Hinata family must find the amulet first. But Hiro still has many **ninja skills** to master. **How can a young ninja-in-training help defeat the most evil ninja in the kingdom?**

The dragons of Asia are quite different. They don't have wings, and their bodies are longer and more snakelike than European dragons. They're not usually thought to be dangerous or evil. Asian dragons are often the guardian spirits of bodies of water, and people believe they can bring good fortune. Today, people in countries such as China and Japan celebrate dragons with special festivals and by performing dragon dances.

In Hiro's Quest, Fujita transforms into a European dragon. He has wings, he can breathe fire, and he is dangerous. The type of dragon he turns into is linked to his evil personality. It is very rare for a ninja to be able to transform into a dragon, but it is likely that some can transform into the more peaceful Asian dragon. It would be interesting to see what would happen if the two types of dragons faced off, wouldn't it?

About Dragons
A Note from the Author

Many cultures around the world tell stories about dragons. The word dragon comes from the Greek word *drakon*, which means "serpent." That's because dragons have long bodies, like snakes.

Descriptions of dragons can be very different, depending on where they come from. In Europe, dragons are said to have large, leathery wings. They usually breathe fire. Europeans feared dragons as dangerous creatures. They were said to guard large hordes of treasure. Anyone who tried to steal a dragon's treasure would be burned to a crisp.

HIRO'S WORLD

Hiro's Quest is a work of fantasy, but it is based on some real ideas and elements from Japan and other places around the world.